JAN BRETT

Gingerbread Baby

JAN BRETT

Gingerbread Baby

SCHOLASTIC INC.
New York Toronto London Auckland Sydney
Mexico City New Delhi Hong Kong

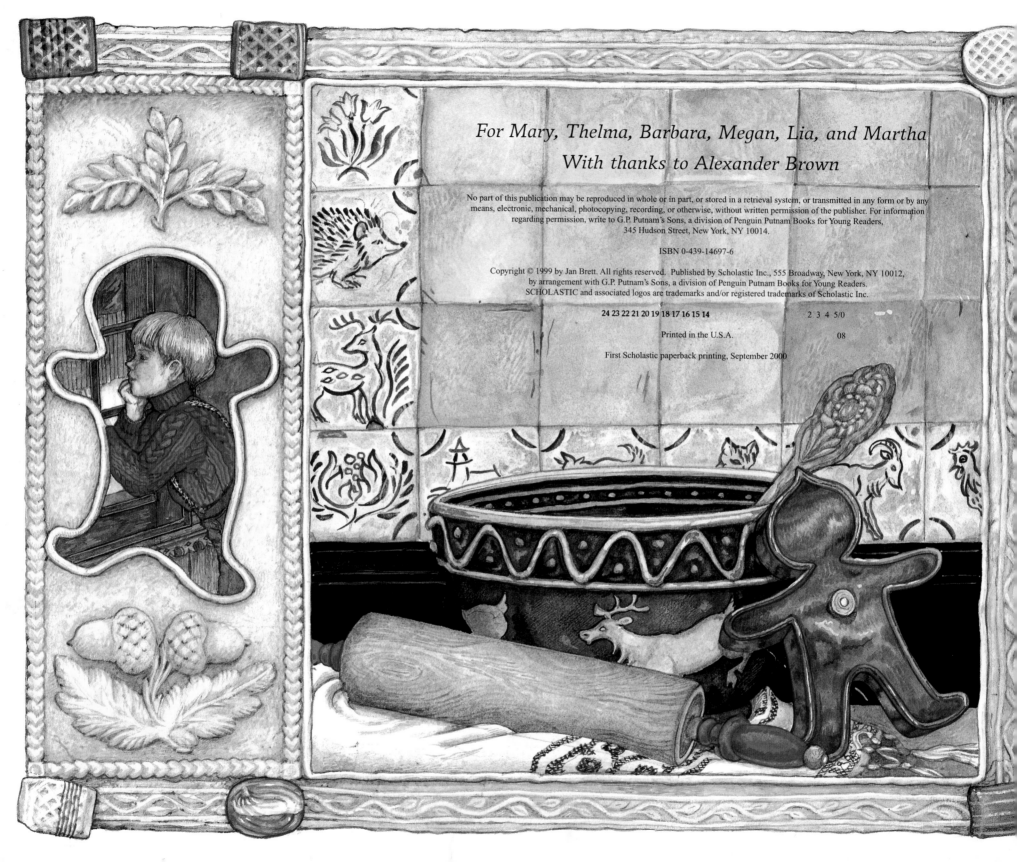

For Mary, Thelma, Barbara, Megan, Lia, and Martha

With thanks to Alexander Brown

ISBN 0-439-14697-6

24 23 22 21 20 19 18 17 16 15 14   2 3 4 5/0

Printed in the U.S.A.   08

First Scholastic paperback printing, September 2000

It was cold outside. It was warm inside. *A fine day for gingerbread,* Matti thought.

Matti's mother put the big blue bowl on the table and lit the stove. Matti took down a worn-looking cookbook with old-fashioned writing on the cover. He opened it up to the page that said "Gingerbread Boy."

They measured and mixed. Matti rolled the dough into the shape of a gingerbread boy and they popped him in the oven. *Bake a full eight minutes. No more. No less. DO NOT peek,* the recipe read.

Matti listened to the clock. Tick, tock, tick. One minute, two minutes, three . . . four . . . five . . . . Matti couldn't wait any longer. He opened the oven door to take a peek. Instead of a gingerbread boy, out jumped a gingerbread baby!

He pranced around the big blue bowl.
"I am the Gingerbread Baby,
Fresh from the pan.
If you want me,
Catch me if you can."

Matti's mother reached for the Gingerbread Baby to put him back into the oven. But he ran all around the kitchen.

The door opened and in came Matti's father. "What's that delicious smell?" he asked as the Gingerbread Baby tumbled through his legs and outside into the yard.

He ran by the tabby cat. She twitched her tail
and sprang at him. They rumbled and tumbled, but
the Gingerbread Baby came out on top.

He ran toward the garden wall. The dog caught a whiff of tasty ginger and sniffed along behind him. But the Gingerbread Baby was halfway up when the dog caught up. He barked and barked as the Gingerbread Baby climbed over the wall.

Matti was still inside. He heard his mother and father yelling. He heard a cat meowing and a dog barking. And he heard the Gingerbread Baby shouting:

"Catch me if you can!"

Matti opened up the worn-looking cookbook for the second time.

Meanwhile the Gingerbread Baby wheeled on down the path and into the barn. The goats looked up as he somersaulted across their backs. The last one tried to catch him, but the Gingerbread Baby was too fast.

Martha and Madeline were standing by the well when the Gingerbread Baby stopped to take a drink. They looked at each other and winked. Martha started to talk to him while Madeline tiptoed up behind him with the bucket. But they couldn't fool that Gingerbread Baby.

He took a braid from Martha and a braid from Madeline
and tied them in a knot and ran down the road.

Back in the house, Matti stirred, mixed and rolled the dough. He shaped it, put it in a pan and into the oven. Tick, tock, tick. Eight long minutes. This time he didn't peek. "I will catch him if I can," Matti said to himself.

As he was bouncing along, the Gingerbread Baby saw a farm wagon just ahead. He jumped in and settled down for the ride next to a mama pig. The smell of gingerbread was too much for her. She tossed him high in the air, closed her eyes and opened her mouth. But the Gingerbread Baby twisted in the air and came down hard on her porky snout.

"I am the Gingerbread Baby.
Too quick for the mother and the father,
Too fast for the cat, the dog, the goats,
Too clever for Martha and Madeline,
Too smart for the mama pig.
Who's left? Catch me if you can!"

Feeling smug, the Gingerbread Baby
strolled along by himself until he came to a bridge
that crossed over to the village. Just as he got to the
middle, he heard running feet behind him and saw a crowd
of villagers ahead of him. The Gingerbread Baby was trapped.
He jumped up onto the railing, backflipped through the air
and landed on a chunk of ice floating down the river.

The ice bobbed along with the Gingerbread Baby
dancing on top, and singing in a loud voice,
"Look at me.
And what do you see?
The best Gingerbread Baby ever!"
Until his feet got cold and he jumped ashore.

Who was that watching from the trees? It was the fox. He crept up behind the Gingerbread Baby, ready to eat him up. But the fox couldn't help himself, and he licked his chops. Smack! Smack! The Gingerbread Baby heard him and ran as fast as he could.

Just when the fox was catching up, the Gingerbread Baby saw the milk and cheese man with his can of milk. *The perfect hiding place,* he thought. He lifted the lid and lowered himself inside. He was so pleased that he sang at the top of his gingerbread voice,

"Ha, ha! Hee, hee!
You'll never find me.
I'm the Gingerbread Baby.
Catch me if you can!"

The milk and cheese man heard the Gingerbread Baby's voice.
"Who is meddling with my milk!" he shouted and lifted the lid. But
the Gingerbread Baby was ready. He jumped up and tweaked his nose.

Now the milk and cheese man, the fox, the villagers, the mama pig, Martha and Madeline, the bleating goats, the barking dog, the meowing cat, the father and the mother were all after the Gingerbread Baby and getting closer.

And he knew it.

The brash baby was not as peppy and proud as he had been. He sniffed a familiar smell and followed his nose into the woods.

He couldn't believe what he saw. There in the middle of a clearing was a gingerbread house, frosted with sugar, covered with candy, and doors with peppermint handles wide open. The Gingerbread Baby clapped his hands with glee and ran inside.

In a tick tock tick, everyone arrived in the clearing, but all they found were a few bits of frosting, a peppermint candy—and some crumbs.

The father exclaimed, "The Gingerbread Baby has finally met his match!"

"I wonder who it was?" the mother said. "Let's go home and tell Matti."

"Hello, Matti," his father said when they got home. "We never did catch that Gingerbread Baby. All we found were some crumbs in the snow."

"I see you have been busy," his mother said, looking at the gingerbread house Matti was holding. "Too bad we never caught that Gingerbread Baby."

"Too bad," said Matti.

Only Matti could hear the tiny voice
from inside the gingerbread house.